WOODCHUCK NATION

by Mark Saltzman
illustrated by Jon Buller

Alfred A. Knopf · New York

THIS IS A BORZOI BOOK PUBLISHED BY ALFRED A. KNOPF, INC.

Text copyright © 1994 by Mark Saltzman
Illustrations copyright © 1994 by Jon Buller

Library of Congress Cataloging-in-Publication Data
Saltzman, Mark.
Woodchuck Nation / by Mark Saltzman ; illustrated by Jon Buller.
  p. cm.
Summary: Zal the woodchuck brings his children to the site of the historic
Woodchuck Festival and describes attending that musical festival twenty-five
years earlier.
ISBN 0-679-85107-0
[1. Music festivals—Fiction. 2. Woodchuck—Fiction.]
I. Buller, Jon, ill. II. Title.
PZ7.S15525Wo 1994   [E]—dc20 93-4641

Manufactured in the United States of America
10 9 8 7 6 5 4 3 2 1

For Arnold and my parents
—M.S.

One warm, beautiful August afternoon, a family of woodchucks—Zal
and May, and their three furry children: Vera, Chook, and Dave—stood
in a gently sloping meadow. They hadn't been there long when the kids
noticed that their dad was acting strange. He kept looking down the
road as if he were waiting for something.

"Daddy, what are you seeing if?" asked Dave, the youngest.

"I'm seeing if someone's coming," said his father.

"Do you want to hear a song while we're waiting?" asked Vera, who
loved to sing.

"Not now, honey," Zal said.

Vera sighed.

Chook was tired of waiting. "Dad, it's time you told us what
we're doing here!" he moaned.

The grown-up woodchucks looked at each other.

"I'll keep watch," May said to Zal. "You tell them."

Zal sat his children down on a boulder. "What I'm going to tell you about," he began, "happened a long time ago—when I was much younger."

"How old were you?" asked Vera.

"Older than you and younger than me," Zal answered. "And back then, the woodchucks of the world decided to have a big outdoor concert with lots of famous musicians. They called it the Woodchuck Festival, and I made plans to go with my good buddy Digger. . . ."

I was so excited! For weeks I had dreams about the festival—swirling, Day-Glo, mystic-crystal dreams about the rock stars I'd be seeing there: Joe Cockatoo, Rabbit Shankar, Jerry Garseagull, and my fave rave, that web-footed wonder of psychedelic guitar, Jimi Hendrake.

And finally the day arrived! When I woke up, I heard the beep of a car horn outside and someone calling my name. "Zal, Zal! Come on! We're ready, man!"

I hopped out of bed, tied back my fur in a headband, and looked at the poster of Jimi Hendrake on the wall. "Jimi, I'm coming," I said. "I'm coming to see you."

My mother, your Grandma Woodchuck, didn't want me to go. She thought the trip would be dangerous. "Please stay home, Zallie," she pleaded. "You know tomorrow's your birthday. I'll make you a beautiful cake, and we'll have our own Woodchuck Festival—right here."

"Oh, ma," I said. "Can't you see? I have to do my own thing in my own time."

"Can't you do your own thing in your own home?" she asked.

Before I could answer, I heard Digger honking again.

"I'll be all right, Ma, I promise," I said, kissing her.

Then I ran out to Digger's van, which everyone called the Chuck Wagon.

Sitting up front with Digger was a woodchuck I'd never met before.

"Zal, man, this is Macra-May," said Digger. "She's gonna make the festival scene with us."

"Cool," I said. Macra-May and I flashed each other the paws sign.

"Three days of paws and music," Macra-May said as we set off.

"Pretty groovy," I said.

"It's beyond groovy, man," shouted Digger. "It's fur out. Dig it?"

"Dug it," said Macra-May.

"Done," I said.

As the Chuck Wagon picked up speed, Macra-May began reading from her book about the stars and planets. "Oh, wow!" she said, "the stars are just right for this festival. The sun is entering the sign of Goopus the Guppy. The moon is between Signo the Snail and Angelus the Angelfish. Surely, this is the dawning of the Age of Aquarium!"

The signs were right for a cosmic happening!

So we grooved along in Digger's funky van, singing with the radio:

"All we are *saaay*-ing

Is give beasts a chance..."

Suddenly the music stopped and a voice broke in.

"Hey, out there," it said. "This is Chip Munk the Chipmunk coming to you from the Woodchuck Festival. Paws and love, brothers and sisters. And to any of you on your way to the scene, we have a special message: Don't do it, man! Turn back! The roads are jammed, and we can't handle the crowds! Turn back!"

"But if the roads are jammed, how are we gonna get there?" I whimpered.

Digger switched off the radio.

"No turning back now," he said.

Soon we saw that Chip Munk the Chipmunk had been telling the truth. There were empty cars lining the road for as far as we could see. There were crowds of travelers on the road, too—woodchucks, squirrels, prairie dogs, and beavers. Everyone looked happy. And everyone was getting along really well, giving each other food, like bark and berries. There was no room to drive, so Digger pulled the Chuck Wagon off the road.

"Bum-MER," Macra-May said, but Digger didn't act like anything was wrong. He just looked at the crowd, shook his head, and said, "This is fan-chuckin'-tastic! Look how everyone's giving stuff away to each other. It's the ultimate love-in! The rising of the cosmic muffin! The true creation of the Woodchuck Nation!"

CHICKEN LITTLE WAS RIGHT!

"But what about the concert?" asked Macra-May. "How are we gonna get there?"

"Here's the plan," said Digger. "We'll leave the Chuck Wagon here. I know these back trails. We'll hike over the mountains to the concert. Dig it?"

"Dug it!" said Macra-May.

"Don't!" I yelped. "Don't tell me you want to hike at night! These mountains are big!"

"Oh, don't be so uptight," said Macra-May.

"Yeah, Zal," said Digger. "Why can't you just let it all hang out?"

"I let SOME of it hang out," I said. "Isn't that enough?"

They both shrugged.

"I'll show them I'm not uptight," I thought, and I packed up my ruck-sack just the way they did, with food, water, and a tent. Then we all set off, hiking to the concert through the big green Cat Skull Mountains.

After a few hours of hiking, we'd finished all our water. And just when we were getting really thirsty, we came to a meadow where some cows were resting near a pond.

"Excuse me, is it cool to drink some water from your pond?" I asked.

"The nerve!" said the biggest cow. "You long-haired rodents come up here and think you can take over our farm! Get your tails out of our meadow!"

"Oh, wow," breathed Macra-May. "This is really messing up my head."

"And all of you are messing up our meadow," said the cow sharply. "Move along now. And while you're at it, get a haircut."

Digger didn't move. Instead, he stared right into the cow's big brown eyes.

"You know, you're looking, but you're not seeing," he said. "You're hearing, but you're not listening. You think we're just long-haired hippie rodents. But we believe in paws and love! And we want to give you something. Here, have some bark and some bayberries."

"And a wildflower," added Macra-May, taking one from behind her ear.

Another, smaller cow walked up. "Oh, heavens, they're sweet kids," she said to the unfriendly cow. "It doesn't matter how long their hair is. Don't you remember when *you* were a calf and you used to kick up your hooves?"

"Oh, all right, then," the first cow said, munching on the flower Macra-May had given her. "Help yourselves to the water." And we dipped right in.

It wasn't long before we had walked all the way up the next mountain, but it still didn't seem as if we were getting any closer to the concert.

Then a big fat raindrop plopped down on my nose. "Oh, *no!*" I yelled. "Rain! Bum-MER!"

"Dig it," said Digger. "Let's climb to the top of that ridge. We'll set up camp there, and the water won't flow down into our tents."

"But aren't we supposed to *go* with the flow?" asked Macra-May.

"At this moment," said Digger, "it's more important to be here now than to go with the flow."

"Zal, what do you think?" asked Macra-May. "Should we be here now, or should we go with the flow?"

"I just want to do the thing that keeps us dry," I said.

"Zal wants to do his thing," said Digger.

"Well, why can't Zal do his thing *and* be here now while we go with the flow?" asked Macra-May.

"Wow, that's heavy," said Digger.

"My TENT is heavy!" I cried. "Let's just climb."

So we set off through the storm to the top of the ridge.

We pitched camp, and I crawled inside my tent, wet and exhausted. I couldn't help thinking that if I'd stayed home I'd be having my birthday party tomorrow. My whole family would be singing, lighting up a cake, and giving me a stack of presents. Instead, I was lying in a tent in the mud, with a hard rain a-fallin'. I dozed off into a sad sleep.

"Zal! Zal!" called Digger, waking me up. "Come out here quick, man!" he shouted. "Hurry!"

I walked out of the tent into the biggest surprise of my life.

The rain had stopped while I was asleep, and in the first light of dawn, I could see thousands of forest creatures, a whole wilderness of them, spread out below us in the field. It was the Woodchuck Festival!

Everyone near our tent was holding up candles. And then they were singing—"Hippie birthday to you! Hippie birthday, dear Zallie…" Digger and Macra-May must've told them all about my birthday while I was asleep.

Surprised? I was blown away! But there was more! Two squirrels gave me a nut cake, some beavers gave me berries and bark, and a Norwegian woodchuck gave me some good Norwegian wood! All these creatures I had never met before were treating me like an old friend!

Then, far off on the stage, somebody appeared holding a guitar.
I couldn't see who it was, but as soon as I heard that first soaring
guitar note, I knew. It was Jimi Hendrake! And he was playing
"Hippie Birthday"! To me!

And wow, my woodchuck mind was blown! I freaked! I nearly chucked wood! Macra-May kissed me on the cheek. "Hippie birthday, Zal," she said.

"Macra-May," I said, "you and Digger were right about coming this way. I'm sorry if I brought you down."

Macra-May smiled sweetly. "Zal," she said. "I am you as you are me and we are furry woodchucks—all together."

Macra-May was so cosmic. Everything was suddenly cosmic. "It's my birthday. It's the Woodchuck Festival. I'll never forget this, not ever!" I cried.

Digger threw open his arms. "Dig it!" he shouted. "I've got a fantastic idea! Let's meet back here again in twenty-five woodland rounds. Whatever we're doing, let's drop it and come back here."

"You think any of this will still be happening then?" I asked.

"We are stardust! We are woodchucks! We are forever! Of *course*
it'll be happening! We'll meet right here, at this very spot. Can
you dig it?"

"Dug it," said Macra-May.

"Done," I said. We smiled at each other and hugged. . . .

"And that's what happened here," Zal finished. "Later on, May and I got married and had you. And you know the rest."

"Dad, how about a song while we wait?" asked Vera.

"Oh, honey, I don't—" Zal began. Then he stopped. "What am I saying?" he exclaimed. "Of course we should have a song. We should have *lots* of songs! A whole festival of them!"

Vera, Chook, and Dave started singing. Soon their parents joined in. The joyful sound of their voices rolled across the meadow, through the trees, and down the road, where a brightly colored van was just slowing to a stop.

The driver stepped out and listened for a moment. "I knew it!" he
cried. "I knew it would still be happening!"

Then Digger ran as fast as he could toward the woodchuck music.